Loveliness

Loveliness
A collection of lyrics and
poetry

Moustafa Fkhir

Your beauty, my lady, is that what kills me
and the longing of my patience
to see you sparked fire inside me

You are the one that made me realise

loving angels is not that easy.

Preface

To all those who are capable of love, are in love or were in love. To all those who love their spouse, partner, children, parents, siblings, friends, colleagues, relatives, neighbours and their pets. To all those who love to live, travel, work, read, have fun and cherish all life moments, the bad and good ones. To all those who believe that love is not a product, currency or a Valentine's Day one thing...

... "Congratulations" for being in such a mesmerising experience, experimenting such a powerful feeling, and enjoying all the bits of love for simply knowing that 'love' is not exclusive to two individuals but for all those around us. For knowing that love is in the air we breathe, in the food we eat, in the simplest of things scattered around our pathways. For knowing that 'love', 'peace' and 'joy' are the true weapons of mass enrichment of one's life, and the fundamental components for creating a 'happy life'.

 With YOU, I share my experience with 'love' and its reflection on my life. Though, I must admit, I am not a poet

nor did I study literature.
Neither did I do that extensive
research on 'HOW TO' write
poetry or read that
Shakespearean magic. But, to
put simply, I am a person 'in
love' and happen to love
'words'.   The below collection is
nothing but a mere attempt of
putting the two together in
some sentences and lines.
 But, if this attempt has taught
me one thing, I now know for
sure that it is so damn hard to
describe 'love'.

        To all those who I love.

 Yours faithfully,
 with love,
 M. Fkhir

Contents

18 reasons for
loving you

I love you because
you are the one who let me go.
I love you because
you're really my soul.
I love you because
you set me free,
you keep me happy,
you challenge me.
Your beauty is breath-taking,
your smile is amazing,
your love is great.
I love you because
I can't really imagine
my life without you
You are my strength
you are my breath
you are everything I could ever
dream.
You are the stars,
you are the moon,

you are all that I wanna die
for.
You are everything
you are my life
I just wanna be beside you
for all my life
All I want, stay next to you
and that's all beside
forever loving you.

I love you because
I simply can't get enough
of loving you.
**

If it wasn't for you

How silly would love be
if it wasn't for you
How empty my life would be
if you weren't my heart beats
How could my day ever be
if you weren't the shine
Lucky me that I'm yours
lucky me that you are mine

Baby, you are the star that
makes my night
you are for whom I sleep
so I can of you dream
I don't wish to close my eyes
if you won't visit me in my
dream
I won't even be alive
if it wasn't for your kiss

Baby, I insanely love you

and for no other love
I worth to remain alive.

***

Love isn't enough

Love doesn't justify
what I feel about you
Passion is not even enough
to describe how insanely I love
you
There are simply no words
that clarify
what I feel toward you

With you I learn how to smile
I hold your hand and fly
I take-over the universe
I feel like I own the sky
I can do anything
next to you I want to die

I will build a nest for us in my
heart
I will lock ourselves in
and lose the keys every night

I will hold your hand
and never ever leave your side

Let's begin our journey
for an endless end
Let's reach out to the stars
and fall in love every second
You are my final destination
where I can live, love and die.

***

An unexpected love

Your beauty is a cause for
admiration
The path to your love
starts with a touch of your
fingers
The warmth of your heart
feels like a fireplace in
Christmas

Your beauty is beyond
description
Are you a queen, a rose or a
ruby?
Are you jasmine, lily or the
delightful smell of blueberry?
whoever you are, I'm sure of
one thing
you are the love that I have
not expected.

***

Valentine's Day

Here is Valentine's Day comes
upon us again
and my heart starts asking me
what will you say to her?

How can you describe love
that stormed your heart like a
hurricane?
How do you describe a delicious
sunflower
to a hungry bee?
How do you describe love
that refurbished your hell
and made it into heaven?

I insanely love her
and it is shamefully unfair
to celebrate her love
just on Valentine's Day.

***

The power of love

It is difficult to hide love
It is impossible to keep it in
disguise
It is that amazing sparkle
that shines everyone's eyes
It is the language that purifies
our hearts
and the craziness we all melt
inside

Love is that powerful weapon
that disarms the most hatred
of minds
The world will be a better
place
if we fire hearts rather than
missiles
One can truly win a war
when the enemies of the past
become your friends for life

Be kind to one another
and let us spread love
all the way.

***

The anniversary

Since the start of our story
no one but you
have the keys to my heart
No one but you
have stolen the wonder of my
thoughts
and to this date, my darling
you still fly like a bird
between my heart and mind

You have taught me the art of
fondness
and changed the laws of love
My eyes start complaining
when you don't come across
their sight
My fingers stop flying
if they don't land in your
hands

If my life was a rollercoaster
being with you
made it a smooth ride.

***

Promise me

Do promise me
that you will never leave my
side
that you will never go away
and throw me to a rich-less
life

Do promise me
that you will always be in my
eyes
and guard all my dreams
and be the light that shines my
path

Please promise me
that we will stay together
forever
and your hands will never
leave mine

You are the port that I will
always sail to
because the safest place on
earth
is right there by your side
So darling do please promise
me
that you will never ever
leave my side.
***

An angel's
birthday

On this day, an angel was born
on the ground
She did not fall from heaven
nor did she ride the rain
to come down from the sky

Please sing for her and dance
because writing poems for her
is not enough
My words stand speechless
in the presence of her charm

Everyone was born for a
reason
and I was born to fall in your
love
You are the answer to my
prayers
You are the coat that keeps me
warm in rainy days

and the book that I want to
read every night

You are the reason behind my
every smile
I so want to hide you forever
between my heart and eyes.

***

Impossible to describe

Are you a butterfly, jewel or a
diamond?
How can one describe your
charm?
You are the masterpiece of love
and the definition of fine art
You are that beautiful song
that is about to be sang
and that Christmas tree
that every family wants to
have
You are that one beautiful star
that sparkles in the dark

Are these good descriptions?
No they are not
No they are not.

***

Crazy jealousness

I am jealous of the winds
blowing into your hair
I am jealous of the perfume
that you always wear
I am jealous from the lipsticks
that are printed on your lips
and I am jealous from that
scarf around your neck

I am jealous
from everything that is around
you
from your clothes hugging you
from the forks, spoons and
knives in your hands
I am even jealous from the
mirrors
if they see you more than my
eyes
I will always be that jealous

because, darling,
you are the beats of my heart
my life's music
and paradise.

***

I won't say:

'The End'

because 'love' is endless.

About the author

My day job involves resolving legal issues arising in the maritime industry, being a newly qualified solicitor interested in ships and what they are used for. My hobby though is writing poetry and crafting the art of 'words'. Mastering the use of words has always fascinated me. As once a wise man or woman said: it is not what you say but the way you say it that matters .. is true! Words can have profounding impact on someone's life, and one can only hope for that impact to be 'positive'.

This is my first attempt in writing poetry in English. It is also my first pieces that I share with the world. I started writing poetry at quite a young age, though all my pieces were in Arabic and for my personal enjoyment. I have hardly shared my pieces with anyone but those that are close to me, or those to whom my pieces were written for.

Certainly, there are always rooms for improvements but I hope you found this collection an enjoyable read !

Keep on loving one another.

M. Fkhir

mfkhir.publications@gmail.com
@mfkhir.publications

CPSIA information can be obtained
at www.ICGtesting.com
Printed in the USA
BVHW060908250321
603396BV00008B/662

9 781838 446802